The First Christmas

The First Christmas

NONNY HOGROGIAN

GREENWILLOW BOOKS, NEW YORK

The passages that appear in italics
are quotations from
the Gospel of Saint Matthew (1:20-21, 2:1-9)
and the Gospel of Saint Luke (1:28-38, 2:7-14)
in the Authorized King James Version
of the Holy Bible.

Oil paints were used for the full-color art. The text type is Leawood Book. Greenwillow Books, a division of William Morrow & Company, Inc., 1350 Avenue of the Americas, New York, NY 10019.
Printed in Hong Kong by South China Printing Company (1988) Ltd. First Edition 10 9 8 7 6 5 4 3 2 1

Library of Congress Cataloging-in-Publication Data
Hogrogian, Nonny. The first christmas / by Nonny Hogrogian. p. cm.
ISBN 0-688-13579-X (trade). ISBN 0-688-13580-3 (lib. bdg.) 1. Jesus Christ—Nativity—Juvenile literature.
2. Bible stories, English—N.T. Gospels. [1. Jesus Christ—Nativity. 2. Bible stories—N.T.] I. Title.
BT315.2.H627 1995 232.92—dc20 94-19367 CIP AC

The wolf also shall dwell with the lamb,
and the leopard shall lie down with the kid;
and the calf and the young lion and the fatling together;
and a little child shall lead them.

—ISAIAH 11:6

This is how it came to pass
that Jesus Christ was born.

The angel Gabriel was sent from God
to a city in Galilee called Nazareth,
to appear before a virgin
betrothed to a man whose name was Joseph.
And the virgin's name was Mary.

The angel appeared before Mary and said,
Blessed art thou among women.

When the angel saw that Mary was troubled,
he said to her,
Fear not, Mary:
for thou hast found favor with God.
And, behold,
thou shalt conceive in thy womb,
and bring forth a son,
and shalt call his name JESUS.

Mary said, "I am a servant of the Lord.
Be it as you will."
And the angel departed from her.

When it was seen that Mary was with child,
the angel of the Lord appeared to Joseph
in a dream, saying,
Joseph, thou son of David,
fear not to take unto thee Mary . . .
for that which is conceived in her
is of the Holy Ghost.
And she shall bring forth a son,
and thou shalt call his name JESUS:
for he shall save his people from their sins.

Joseph did as the angel had bidden him

and took Mary for his wife.

There came a time that Mary and Joseph
needed to travel to Bethlehem
to pay their taxes,
and Mary was great with child.

And it was in Bethlehem
that Mary brought forth her firstborn son.
She *wrapped him in swaddling clothes,
and laid him in a manger;
because there was no room for them
in the inn.*

Not far from where the child was born,
there were shepherds tending their flocks.
The angel of the Lord came to them,
and the glory of the Lord
shone round about them. . . .
And the angel said unto them, Fear not:
for, behold, I bring you good tidings
of great joy, which shall be to all people.
For unto you is born this day
in the city of David a Savior,
which is Christ the Lord.
And this shall be a sign unto you;
Ye shall find the babe
wrapped in swaddling clothes,
lying in a manger.

And suddenly there was with the angel
a multitude of the heavenly host
praising God, and saying,
Glory to God in the highest,
and on earth peace,
good will toward men.

The shepherds made their way to Bethlehem,
where they found Mary and Joseph
with their babe, who was lying in a manger.
And when they departed, they spread the word
of the angel of the Lord.

Now when Jesus was born . . .
there came wise men from the east
to Jerusalem, saying . . .
we have seen his star in the east,
and are come to worship Him.

. . . and, lo, the star, which they saw
in the east, went before them,

till it came and stood
over where the young child was.
When they saw the babe
with Mary, his mother,

they fell down and they worshiped him,
and they presented him with gifts
of gold and frankincense and myrrh.

Glory to God in the highest,
and on earth peace,
good will toward men.

Hiram Halle Memorial Library
Pound Ridge, New York